The Open Road

from
The Wind in the Willows

Written by
KENNETH GRAHAME

Abridged and illustrated by
INGA MOORE

TED SMART

The Open Road

"Ratty," said the Mole suddenly, one bright summer morning. "Please, I want to ask you a favour."

The Rat was sitting on the river bank, singing a little song he had just composed about ducks, which he called

DUCK'S DITTY

All along the backwater,
Through the rushes tall,
Ducks are a-dabbling,
Up tails all!

Ducks' tails, drakes' tails,
Yellow feet a-quiver,
Yellow bills all out of sight
Busy in the river!

Everyone for what he likes!
We like to be
Heads down, tails up,
Dabbling free!

"I don't know that I think so *very* much of that little song, Rat," observed the Mole. He was no poet himself and didn't care who knew it. "But what I wanted to ask you was, won't you take me to call on Mr Toad?"

"Why, certainly," said the Rat, jumping to his feet. "Get the boat out at once. It's never the wrong time to call on Toad. He's always glad to see you, always sorry when you go!"

"He must be a very nice animal," observed the Mole, as he got into the boat and took the sculls.

"He is the best of animals," replied Rat. "Perhaps he's not very clever and it may be that he is boastful and conceited. But he has some great qualities, has Toady."

Rounding a bend in the river, they came in sight of Toad Hall, a handsome, dignified old house of mellowed red brick with well-kept lawns reaching down to the water's edge.

They left the boat in the boat-house, and went to look up Toad, whom they happened upon in a wicker garden-chair, a large map spread out on his knees.

"Hooray!" he cried, jumping up. "This is splendid!" He shook their paws. "How *kind* of you! I was just going to send a boat down the river for you, Ratty. I want you badly – both of you."

"It's about your rowing, I suppose," said the Rat. "You're getting on fairly well, and with coaching—"

"O, pooh! boating!" interrupted the Toad. "I've given that up *long* ago. No, I've discovered the real thing! Come with me and you shall see what you shall see!"

He led the way to the stable-yard and there, drawn out of the coach-house, they saw a gipsy caravan, shining with newness, painted a canary-yellow picked out with green, and red wheels.

"There you are!" cried the Toad, straddling and expanding himself. "There's real life for you. The open road, the dusty highway, the heath, the common, the rolling downs! Here today, and off somewhere else tomorrow! The whole world before you! And mind, this is the finest cart of its sort ever built."

The Mole followed him eagerly up the steps and into the caravan. It was very compact and comfortable. Little sleeping-bunks – a table that folded up against the wall – a cooking-stove, lockers, bookshelves and pots, pans, jugs and kettles of every size and variety.

"You see – " said the Toad, pulling open a locker, "biscuits, potted lobster, sardines – everything you can possibly want. Soda-water here – letter-paper there, bacon, jam, cards and dominoes – you'll find," he continued, "that nothing has been forgotten, when we make our start this afternoon."

"I beg your pardon," said the Rat, "but did I hear you say 'we', and 'start', and 'this afternoon'?"

"Dear Ratty," said Toad, "you've *got* to come. I can't manage without you. You don't mean to stick to your river all your life."

"I *am* going to stick to my river," said the Rat. "And what's more, Mole's going to stick to me, aren't you, Mole?"

"I'll always stick to you, Rat," said the Mole loyally. "All the same, it sounds as if it might have been – well, fun!" Poor Mole! He had fallen in love at first sight with the canary-coloured cart and all its little fitments.

The Rat saw what was in his mind and wavered. He was fond of the Mole, and would do almost anything to oblige him. Toad was watching them closely.

"Come along in and have some lunch," he said, "and we'll talk it over. We needn't decide anything in a hurry."

During lunch the Toad simply let himself go, painting the joys of the open life and roadside in such glowing colours that the Mole could hardly sit in his chair for excitement. Somehow, it seemed taken for granted that the trip was a settled thing; and the good-natured Rat could not bear to disappoint his two friends, who were already planning each day for several weeks ahead. The triumphant Toad led his companions to the paddock, and set them to capture the old grey horse, who, to his extreme annoyance, had been told off by Toad for the dustiest job in this expedition. He frankly preferred the paddock, and took a deal of catching. At last he was caught and harnessed and they set off, all talking at once, each animal either trudging by the side of the cart or sitting on the shaft, as the humour took him. It was a golden afternoon. The smell of the dust they kicked up was rich and satisfying; out of orchards on either side the road, birds called and whistled to them cheerily, wayfarers, passing them, gave them "Good day," or stopped to say nice things about their beautiful cart; and rabbits, sitting at their front doors in the hedgerows, held up their fore-paws, and said, "O my!"

Late in the evening, tired and happy and miles from home, they drew up on a remote common, turned the horse loose to graze, and ate their supper sitting on the grass by the side of the cart. Toad talked big about all he was going to do in the days to come, while stars grew fuller all around them …

and a yellow moon, appearing from nowhere in particular,

came to keep them company and listen to their talk.

At last they turned into their little bunks; and Toad, kicking out his legs, sleepily said, "Well, good night, you fellows! This is the life! Talk about your old river!"

"I *don't* talk about my river," replied the Rat. "You *know* I don't, Toad. But I *think* about it," he added. "I *think* about it all the time!" The Mole reached out from under his blanket, felt for the Rat's paw in the darkness, and gave it a squeeze. "Shall we run away tomorrow," he whispered, " – *very* early – and go back to our dear old hole on the river?"

"No, we'll see it out," whispered back the Rat. "I ought to stick by Toad till this trip is ended. It wouldn't be safe for him to be left to himself. It won't take very long. His fads never do."

The end was nearer than even the Rat suspected.

The Toad slept very soundly, and no amount of shaking could rouse him out of bed next morning. So the Mole and Rat turned to, and while the Rat saw to the horse, and lit a fire, and got things ready for breakfast, the Mole trudged off to the nearest village, a long way off, for milk and eggs, which the Toad had, of course, forgotten. The two animals were thoroughly exhausted by the time Toad appeared, fresh and gay, remarking what a pleasant easy life they were leading now, after the cares and worries of housekeeping at home.

They had a pleasant ramble that day over grassy downs, and camped, as before, on a common, only this time the guests took care that Toad should do his share of the work. Next morning their way lay across country by narrow lanes, and it was not till the afternoon that they came out on their first high road; and there disaster sprang out on them.

They were strolling along, the Mole by the horse's head, since the horse had complained that he was being left out of it; the Toad and the Water Rat walking behind the cart talking – at least Toad was talking, and Rat was saying at intervals, "Yes, and what did *you* say to *him*?" – and thinking all the time of something very different, when behind them they heard a warning hum, like the drone of a bee. Glancing back, they saw a small cloud of dust, with a dark centre of energy, advancing on them at incredible speed, while from out of the dust wailed a faint "Poop-poop!"

In an instant the peaceful scene was changed. The "poop-poop" rang with a brazen shout in their ears, and with a blast of wind and a whirl of sound that made them jump for the nearest ditch, the motor-car – its pilot tense and hugging his wheel – was on them. It flung a cloud of dust that blinded them utterly, and then dwindled to a speck in the far distance.

The old grey horse, rearing, plunging, backing steadily, in spite of all the Mole's efforts at his head, drove the cart backwards towards the side of the road. It wavered – then there was a heart-rending crash – and the canary-coloured cart lay on its side in a deep ditch.

"You villains!" shouted the Rat, shaking both fists. "You scoundrels, you – you – road-hogs!"

Toad sat in the middle of the road, his legs stretched out before him, his eyes fixed on the dusty wake of the motor-car. He breathed short, and at intervals murmured "Poop-poop!"

The Mole was trying to quiet the horse. The Rat came to help him. "Hi, Toad!" they cried. "Bear a hand, can't you!"

The Toad never budged. He was in a sort of trance, a happy smile on his face. "The *real* way to travel!" he murmured. "The *only* way to travel! O bliss! O poop-poop! And to think I never *knew*, never even *dreamt*! But *now* – now I know! What dust-clouds shall spring up behind me as I speed on my way! What carts I shall fling into the ditch! Horrid carts – common carts – canary-coloured carts!"

"What are we to do with him?" asked the Mole.

"Nothing," replied the Rat. "You see, I know him of old. He has got a new craze and it always takes him that way, like an animal in a happy dream, quite useless. Never mind him. Let's see about the cart."

A careful inspection showed them that the cart would travel no longer. The axles were in a hopeless state, and one wheel was shattered into pieces.

The Rat took the horse by the head. "Come on!" he said to the Mole. "We shall just have to walk to the nearest town."

"But what about Toad?" asked the Mole.

"O, *bother* Toad," said the Rat.

They had not proceeded very far, however, when there was a pattering of feet behind them, and Toad caught them up.

"Now, look here, Toad!" said the Rat: "as soon as we get to the town, you'll go straight to the police-station, and lodge a complaint against that motor-car."

"Complaint! Me *complain* of that beautiful, heavenly vision! That swan, that sunbeam, that thunderbolt!"

The Rat turned from him in despair. "I give up," he said.

On reaching the town they went straight to the station and deposited Toad in the second-class waiting-room, giving a porter twopence to keep a strict eye on him. They left the horse at an inn stable, and gave what directions they could about the cart. Eventually, a slow train having landed them not far from Toad Hall, they escorted the spellbound Toad to his door. Then they got out their boat and sculled down the river, and at a very late hour sat down to supper in their own cosy parlour.

The following evening the Mole, who had taken things easy all day, was sitting on the bank fishing, when the Rat came strolling along to find him. "Heard the news?" he said. "There's nothing else being talked about, all along the river bank. Toad went up to Town by an early train this morning. And he has ordered a large and very expensive motor-car."